K.C. CORDELL

You obviously have highly discerning taste…

And if this weirdness is right up your alley, then you should definitely sign up to receive updates on upcoming books, behind-the-scene sneak peeks, and various chitchat from the author.

www.kccordell.com/newsletter

Dedicated to my awesome family who has been amazingly, stupendously, fantabulously supportive.

To the friends and family who read so much of my writing (not all of it spectacular) that came before this.

And to my nieces and nephews who inspire me everyday.

SO YOU SURVIVED THE END OF THE WORLD

LIFE after the end of the world ain't so bad when you got the right music.

And that's why Sebastian Yun queues up Queen.

"Next up on *So You Survived the End of the World*," he says, knowing the mic in his data cuff captures every word, "a solid hour from one of my all-time favorite bands. 'Cuz you done earned it, my loyal listeners. For making it one more day in this living hell we humbly call home. But first, what's this?"

He sits a little straighter. Or as close to straight as he's willing to get without sacrificing his deep slouch into the generous cushion of the large passenger seat. Not moving is his current life choice.

His insides are no longer attempting a coup as they had been when he dragged himself up this morning, and his head's no longer pounding like the pissed off drummer of an especially aggro metal band. Still, not moving is pretty awesome.

"Doth my eyes deceive me," he asks his listeners, rhetorically of course, "or do we have us a caller?"

The blinking notification on his round holo-interface doesn't go away. It isn't a trick of his eyes, and maybe not even a weird glitch.

"Well, ain't that a treat?"

From day one, he's had a standing policy to take every caller he gets. They're too rare for him not to. Rare, as in this is the very first time it has ever happened.

He has plenty of listeners out there. He knows that much from the welcome—good and bad—he receives every time he pulls up to a town in his distinctive ride.

But even as more and more people in the Midlands tune in, folks still tend to be a bit gun shy when it comes to the casual use of technology. Something about tech's role in the fall of civilization rubs people the wrong way. So they listen, but actively transmitting a signal out is a bridge too far for most.

Sebastian flicks the flashing icon on his holo-interface, allowing the maybe-a-caller-maybe-a-glitch to join the live broadcast.

"Howdy do, listener?"

"H-hi, Sebastian," says the actual caller and definitely not a glitch.

Sebastian is tempted to not only sit up straight, but to do a little happy dance. But then he remembers his whole not moving agenda. He settles for a wide grin instead.

"Got a name?"

"Yes."

Sebastian waits.

Crickets.

"So this here's a guessing game, eh?" Sebastian says. "Alrighty…Adam. Kenny. Bobby. Larry. Curly. Moe. We might be here a while, but I'm sure the listeners are riveted."

"Oh, sorry. J-Johnny."

"So, J-Johnny. Calling in to tell me what a kick-ass job I been doing? Or you got something you wanna share with all the fine folks out there?"

"Well, I been thinking an awful lot."

"Uh-oh."

"Pardon?"

"I said, please, tell me what's been keeping you up at night. You know, besides the fact that everything on this godforsaken planet is actively trying to exterminate the human race."

Feet kicked up on the dashboard, Sebastian reclines in the second best seat that exists anywhere in this sad excuse for a world: the passenger chair he'd installed on Her Royal Majesty, his lovingly and painstakingly restored double decker tour bus.

Of course, the very best seat that exists anywhere in this sad excuse for a world is directly to the left of him. Nothing beats the view from behind the wheel of HRM as she devours the road. But when they're parked and settled for a day or two, Sebastian likes to stretch out his legs while doing a show. So second best seat it is.

"Well—" J-Johnny says. "Um… I mean—uh…Sorry."

"Take your time, J-Johnny. Putting yourself out there to a bunch of strangers takes balls." Sebastian's first broadcast had been fueled by what Meza would have called an unhealthy amount of liquid courage. Had she been around at that time. "Besides, what are the good listeners gonna do? Turn to the other only radio show out there?"

"All my life, I been a'wandering…"

"Yeees?"

"Why'd I have to come into the world after the fall of our greatest civilization? Why I gotta deal with savage hellions and bodysnatching sludgebrains and conniving flatliners?"

The warmth leeches from Sebastian. His stomach turns to stone.

It's just a word.

Push it away.

"Why do we all bother fighting so hard to make it through each miserable day?"

"I hear you," Sebastian says, thoughtful. "But counterargument. Why not?" He shrugs even though no one can see him.

"This is the worst time in history to be alive," J-Johnny barrels over Sebastian's contribution. The guy has finally found his nerve. Good for him. "Our grandparents' grandparents didn't know nothing about hunger, illness, violence. They lived in big ol' cities that catered to their every whim. Our ancestors built *utopia*."

The dusty town on the other side of HRM's giant windshield is a far cry from the fabled cities of old. Talk about going back to square one. The shabby collection of structures behind an admittedly impressive, patchwork metal wall probably doesn't hold enough people to be called a town. If anyone wanted to get technical about it.

Sebastian wonders if its tiny population made it a village. Technically speaking.

No. Too medieval.

Hamlet?

Definitely not. That made it sound entirely too cute.

J-Johnny is still talking.

And sobbing?

"…And it was your show—listening to you everyday done helped me realize all of this. Thank you, Sebastian Yun. Thank you. Because of you, I got purpose like I ain't ever had before."

"Right, right," Sebastian mumbles. "I was totally listening the whole time. Didn't miss a word. But for the folks out there who weren't paying attention—shame on them—repeat that whole thing. Sorta from the beginning."

"I—I said that I understand our purpose now. Because one day we're gonna get back to what we had. We already started rebuilding civilization. I mean, a little. So it's only a matter of time before we get utopia back. I probably won't ever see it, but I can keep fighting. Not for me. For the future."

Sebastian unmutes his mic, which he'd had to silence when he failed to stifle a great big yawn. "Well, this is awkward."

"What?"

"I get the feeling you're waiting for me to co-sign, but that just ain't gonna happen. My apologies."

"But…ain't that why you broadcast your show? To remind us all that we were once great and can be again?"

"Not even kinda."

"But… But…"

"I sense your brain is having a hard time with this, J-Johnny, so let me explain the world to you as it actually is. Might be hard to hear, but it'll save you a whole bunch of heartache in the long run. You might wanna grab something to write with. You got something to write with, J-Johnny?"

"Um…"

"Here it is. The super important conclusion I done reached about our place in all of this. You ready?"

"Uh…"

"That whole perfect civilization thing, it was a blip in the way things always have been and will be for us humans. You got more in common with most of mankind throughout history than those pampered utopians ever did. We weren't meant to live perfect, easy lives. That's all there is to it. And if we lie down and give up, wouldn't it be a big slap in the face to all the generations that came before us and survived their versions of hell on Earth so that we'd have a chance to do the same?"

"Then why you broadcast your music everyday?"

Sebastian shrugs to no one again. "I like music."

"But—But that ain't enough."

"Ain't enough? That's everything. That is the most stupendous nugget of insight you could ever hope to receive. Feel free to pour on the gratitude."

J-Johnny's silence does not feel like the grateful type.

"Heavy sigh. Let's make us a deal, J-Johnny. How about we stop dwelling on what once was and live for today? Why not steal bits of happiness where we can, you know? Find joy in the little things. Because, yeah, most of us will probably suffer horrible, bloody, untimely deaths, but does that mean we can't live it up in the meanwhile?"

"I guess not."

"Darn tootin.' And listen, J-Johnny. In about two seconds, I'm giving you a solid hour of Queen. One of the greatest rock bands to ever grace this planet. Then, tomorrow, on top of my Anything Goes block and the Most Requested hour, you gonna get a bangin' block from Rick the Ruler himself. That's right. Slick freakin' Rick. Then the day after that, we'll see what happens. Maybe we'll take a deep dive into the Best of Bollywood. And I know Kumar Sanu singing Chand Sitare hits you in the feels just like it does me. Does it not?"

"It does."

"If that ain't worth surviving another day for, I don't know what is."

"Building a brighter future for the next generation?"

"Pssh! Let's focus on things that can actually happen. Like you tuning in tomorrow. You gonna tune in tomorrow, J-Johnny?"

"I guess."

"You guess? I reckon you don't quite comprehend how

many hours I put into curating these here playlists. All so that your ears are treated only to the best of the best of all the music in all of existence. Here's a hint. A hell of a lot. So I'm gonna ask you again. Are you tuning in tomorrow?"

"Yes."

"I didn't hear that. Are you tuning in tomorrow?"

"Yes!"

"And the day after tomorrow?"

"Yes!"

"And what about the day after that?"

"I'll be listening, Sebastian."

"Damn right, you will. Now. Any shout-outs?"

"What is a shout-out?"

Sebastian is used to people having no idea what he's talking about, but he sighs anyway. It isn't easy being born in the entirely wrong century.

"By the way," he says to his unseen audience after disconnecting with J-Johnny, "those cities turned against humanity in the end, so they couldn't have been all that great. Those uptopians did know how to build a lasting infrastructure, though. I guess you oughta thank them for access to the data streams, otherwise your lives woulda been sadly devoid of this gem… "

He flicks an icon and the snippet of an Old World song plays. A high feminine voice sings that she's a doll while a deep male voice invites her to party.

"Barbie Girl" stays queued up on Sebastian's sound clips. Because he knows what the people need.

"And speaking of reasons to live," he says after the seconds-long clip ends, "if you're near the charming… *town* of Hope today, be sure to swing by and check out my Itty-Bitty Carnaval de Mécanique Curios, a limited time attraction set up just for you, by me. You're welcome very much. Which charming town of Hope, you ask? Good question.

Not like every place out here didn't decide to call itself 'Hope'. It seems people think that if they keep using the name, more of it will magically appear."

Sebastian taps the door at his side, prompting it to slide open.

"Meza!" he calls out, placing a hand over his data cuff to block the mic. "Hey, Meza!"

"What?" her muffled shout comes from somewhere outside Her Royal Majesty.

"Which charming town of Hope is this again?"

"What?"

"Where. Are. We?" Sebastian hollers, even louder.

"What?" She sounds irritated. But what's new?

"Never mind!" Lowering his voice, he addresses his audience again. "I'll hafta get back to you about our exact location, fellow post-apocalyptizens. Or just look for Her Royal Majesty. Can't miss us. Now, here's 'Don't Stop Me Now'. But try telling that to a hellion. Ha."

Before dismissing the holo-interface, Sebastian turns off his mic and starts the Queen playlist he'd put together last night. It really had taken him hours to decide which songs to include and which to leave out. Not an easy task by any measure.

Clambering out of HRM through the front door takes a bit of skillful maneuvering, especially with an NX-84 Waster holstered at the hip, and a literal leap of faith every time.

The former band tour bus hadn't included a passenger seat for a reason, as Meza had pointed out when he'd giddily installed it. And putting in the tall seat had taken up the space of what should have been an unimpeded entrance to HRM. But whatever, they make it work.

"Hey, Meza!" After leaping out of the bus, Sebastian secures his second weapon across his back. An 18-inch FT-K Devastator he christened "Captain". "What do you call a place too small to be considered a town, but too not-cute to be called a hamlet?"

"That what you were bugging me about?"

Sebastian digs a data ring out of his pockets. It's small, and limited compared to capabilities of a data cuff, but it's pre-configured to receive his broadcast. He flicks on the device and is rewarded with the reinvigorating sounds of Queen. Setting the ring on a nearby tablet, he meanders in the direction of Meza's voice.

An enormous, roll out awning extends from the double-decker bus, casting a generous pool of shade. Though the air's so hot and dry it barely makes a difference.

There's no good weather anymore. Not in the vast majority of the Midlands, at least. Sebastian has watched Old World shows and movies that take place during spring and autumn, but they only get two seasons in these parts. If Sebastian's skin isn't tanned and rough from too much sun and dust, it—at least for a brief period of the year—is red and rough from too much cold and sleet.

Laid out across several small tables in the shade, the Itty-Bitty Carnaval de Mécanique Curios is a roaring success. Only a few townspeople—hamletspeople? Nope, doesn't sound right the moment Sebastian thinks it—mill about in the shade. It's mostly kids. But considering how everyone here is in constant "work is survival, survival is work" mode, this tiny crowd in the middle of the day has exceeded his expectations.

The children of Hope laugh and point at the tiny, ancient mechanical animals that make up Sebastian's Carnaval. Each critter whirs with motion on its own little light up platform.

A seal bobs up and down with a ball balanced on its nose. An elephant rises up on its hind legs, falls back to all fours, then rises up again. A dog chases its own tail in an endless circle. There are twenty-two in total. Each one a unique, handcrafted masterpiece no bigger than a toddler's fist, created back when people wasted time and talent on useless things.

Sebastian hits pause on his search for Meza when a small troop of young ladies venture through the big, open gates of the town—that's so the wrong word for this place. He strolls away from the small collection of tables to meet them.

As he approaches, he oh-so-casually rakes a hand through dark hair overdue for a haircut. It's a gesture that draws attention to what, in his humble opinion, are biceps worthy of a little attention. He may or may not have spent some time posing in front of his reflection to confirm this.

"Well, hello there, Jo, Winona, Hope, Hope, and Hope. Ain't you all the prettiest girls I ever did see."

With an eye roll, Meza is usually quick to point out that he says every girl he meets is the prettiest he's ever seen. But this time it really is true. Or maybe the girls of the world *are* getting prettier. Has Meza thought of that? Who are they to say it isn't happening? Neither of them are scientists.

"Hi, Bazzy," the girls chorus sweetly, all coy smiles and glances through eyelashes. Or at least, mostly all.

Blonde, a little thick, and impassive, Hope #3 meets Sebastian's gaze. "You used that line yesterday."

His grin widens. "Don't make it any less true."

He'd crossed paths with her several times in the previous day. With the population behind those walls so minuscule, how could he not? During each encounter, regardless of what was happening around her, she'd worn the same inscrutable expression that she wears now.

Alas, what is it about unsmiling girls that causes his heart to pitter-patter so?

With a grand wave, he pivots back toward the Carnaval. "Step right on up. Feast your eyes on mechanical whimsy and genius the likes of which you have never before seen."

"Hm." Hope #3 spares the curios a cursory glance.

"Lemme guess," Sebastian says. "This ain't stirring much excitement in you, Miss Hope."

"Nothing personal. Ain't much that impresses me."

"Sounds like a challenge."

Her eyes travel languidly down the length of him and back up again. Aloof as ever, she arches an eyebrow. "Perhaps it is."

Sebastian's smile grows even broader. Challenge accepted.

On the opposite side of the Carnaval, a set of mechanical animals inexplicably go still, the lights of their platforms blinking out. The kids crowded around the display "Aaaw" their disappointment.

Sebastian spots Meza by her dark halo of textured hair poking out from behind the table in question.

"Pardon me," he says. "I need a quick second here."

Tucked behind the table, Meza holds the Sol canister that, up until a few second ago, had been rigged up to power the now immobile set of mechanical animals.

"Hey, lady," says a boy about ten with about fifteen pounds of dirt caked into his clothes. A handful of other runts of various ages stand around him, the obvious ring-leader. Brows furrowed and fists on hips, between them they must have a hundred pounds of dust to shake out of their weathered clothing at the end of each day.

"Why'd you have to do that for?" the boy says. "We were looking at it."

Meza doesn't hide her grimace before angling her back to them. She's never particularly cared for the company of children. Sebastian imagines that even when she was knee high herself, all she had for other kids when they invited her to play in the dirt was the same scowl she arms herself with today. Though it's not that hard to picture.

She barely stands taller than some of these kids. Not that Sebastian would ever make the mistake of insinuating that she's adorable. Again. Just like he would never be tempted to use her head as an armrest when he's standing next to her. Even though the top of her head is at the perfect height for exactly that.

"Hey, lady," Sebastian says, standing behind the kids. "Why'd you have to do that for?"

Rising, but still not acknowledging the runts, Meza frowns at the gauge indicating that the Sol canister is half-depleted of its stored energy. Standing on the opposite side of the table where the awning's shade falls short, she's left fully at the mercy of the sun. Sweat beads on her dark skin. She's only seventeen, a year younger than Sebastian, but she might be the most brilliant tech head he's ever met.

She turns her frown on Sebastian. "Quit wasting the Sols on these things."

"Not even this cute mécanique dog chasing his own tail? Look at the little retro guy go." He leans over the neighboring table where the dog is still going at it. "You'll never get it, buddy. You're trapped in a vicious cycle."

The kids gather around the second table, giggling. At least someone out here finds him amusing.

"No," Meza says.

"What?" Sebastian cries, throwing up his arms. "Why not? You're being completely unreasonable!"

"Need them to make the bus run when we've been without sun."

He gestures toward the relentlessly cloudless sky. "When does that ever happen?"

"Every night."

"Well…"

In that case, she wouldn't be happy to hear that he'd traded two canisters for this mechanical menagerie. But it's her fault for being so good with tech. He has full confidence that if it really came down to it, she'd be able to whip a couple Sols up from scratch. And intimidate the sun into shining at midnight while she's at it.

"You squander too much power on silly things, like pointless toys."

"Uh, first of all, the point of toys are to be pointless. Secondly," he gestures toward the kids, "look at these adorable little faces and tell me a little power ain't worth it."

She doesn't look at the adorable little faces. "Ain't worth it."

"Relax, Meza," Sebastian says, pulling the narrow canister from her hands. "There're plenty of Sols to go around."

"There *were* plenty. 'Til you were unleashed on our reserves. Now, we gotta replenish our supply, quick, or trade for more. And since you insist on giving our refurbed data rings away—"

"How else will people listen to my show?"

"—what we got to spare right now that's worth trading?"

Sebastian balances the Sol upright on his palm. It teeters on its rounded end. "There's always my charm and good looks, but I ain't figured out how to bottle those yet."

Meza snatches the canister back. "I'm being serious."

"I know! That's why it's so hard to keep a straight face."

Considering she has her own set of blasters, a matching NX-84 in a shoulder holster and a 16-inch FT-M Devastator strapped to her leg, a smarter man would think twice about antagonizing her. But he never claimed to be the brains of their operation.

"Sebastian Yun!" a grizzled voice calls out.

Sebastian groans. This guy again.

He knows that he's supposed to revere elders. Hardly anyone makes it to the wrinkled and gray stage of life. But if people get this annoying when they get up there in age, maybe monsters aren't the real reason there's so few old folks around.

"You oughta be ashamed," the old man says by way of greeting, dry, crinkly lips turned down in disgust.

"And good afternoon to you, as well."

"You're an irresponsible jackass."

Sebastian tilts his head, considering. "Fair."

The kids "Aaaw" again as Meza disconnects a Sol canister from another table.

"Broadcasting your brainless dribble drabble for hours everyday," the old man says. "And for what? So you can hear yourself talk foolishness and pump that garbage out for anybody—any*thing* to catch wind of. You go around corrupting otherwise sensible men and women. Getting them to thinking it's okay to use them data rings all day everyday with no regard to the trouble it'll bring. There's a reason we left the Old World tech in the past— "

"Correct me if I'm wrong," Sebastian says, "but that well-used vehicle I noticed tucked behind your walls, that's tech, huh? And them blasters you all cling to, that's something we got thanks to the Old Worlders, right?" He flicks up a finger as he goes down the list. "Your radios, and lights, and water purification system, and don't tell me y'all ain't got a data hoop squirreled away somewhere in there. For emergencies, of course."

"Ain't the same."

"Well, elder, you're as charming as a barrel of hungry hellions and I hate to cut this short—"

"I got something important for you to announce on your little show."

"Sorry. Only foolishness and or garbage allowed. Gotta keep standards up, you know."

"Shut your trap and listen. A holy woman been roaming around these parts for weeks now, going from town to town.

She got some kinda power to drive out the evil hellions! I hear tell she can even separate sludgebrains from them nasty parasites that done crawled up into their noggins. I pray every day that she comes visit us here."

Another Carnaval table goes still. Meza shoots the protesting children a withering glare.

"Does this woman also live in a bottle and grant wishes?" Sebastian asks. "I could really use a less uptight sidekick."

"Bite me," Meza says. "And I ain't your sidekick."

The old man shakes his head vehemently. "No, no, no. This holy woman is the real deal. My neighbor's nephew's girlfriend saw it with her own two eyes. Come hear her tell it!"

"Your neighbor's nephew's girlfriend... Right. Sounds super legit to me."

"You young whippersnappers think you know everything. Never wanna listen. I been around since before the hellions' portals ever opened!"

Sebastian purses his lips. Why is it that every old person tries to claim they witnessed the fall of civilization with their own two eyes? As if math isn't a thing.

"That would make you like a billion years old, and you hardly look a day over one hundred and five."

The old man turns red all the way from his neck to his hairline. "I survived the end of the world, and I'm still alive and kicking. In my day, the young folk knew how to show respect. When our elders told us to do something, we jumped to it. 'Course, back then, following a command was a matter of life or death. This generation done got too soft. You think just 'cuz we established a little stability for you—"

"Okay, old timer. I'll say I believe you if it means I can skip the geezer lecture."

Meza gives Sebastian a disapproving look.

"What?" he asks. "It's okay for you to kill the joy of children but I can't be honest when addressing the elderly?"

"This gotta be a scam," she says, pulling him aside. "Guessing whoever this lady is, she ain't offering her services for free."

"Oh, yeah," Sebastian laughs. "Definitely some kind of racket. Well, you know what they say. There's one born every minute."

"We gotta do something."

He cocks his head, narrows his eyes at her. "Why?"

"Folks in these parts ain't got much. Can't let some charlatan take 'em for everything. We gotta learn more so you can put out a warning about her on your show."

"Or—and just hear me out, here—we don't."

"Sebastian—"

"Times are tough. This woman's trying to make her way in the world same as the rest of us. Who are we to deprive her of her livelihood if these people are dumb enough to fall for it?"

Meza glares at him.

"No?" he says. "Okay. How about this, then? It's an even exchange of goods. These people want hope and she's selling it to 'em at competitive rates."

Meza sidesteps Sebastian to address the old man. "Elder…"

"You can call me Carl."

"Got to put a few things away, Elder Carl, then we'll come inside and talk to your neighbor's girlfriend."

"My neighbor's *nephew's* girlfriend."

"Right. Her."

Sebastian groans heavily as Meza disconnects the remaining Sols. "I'm flattered you think I'm capable of evolving into a better person—"

"What? By reminding you to care about human beings who ain't you?"

"Yes! That very nonsense! But, one day, you're gonna hafta accept that this is who I am. A shallow but rakishly gorgeous guy with awesome taste in music."

After putting the Sols away, Meza offers her arm to the old man. They stroll together toward the wall's gate.

Her Royal Majesty is too big to make it through the opening, and even if they did get it inside, it would take up the entirety of the tiny "town" square. Sebastian and Meza had been forced to park outside Hope. But that's the way it usually went with small places like this.

Borough, maybe?

Too metropolitan.

Sebastian trails behind Meza and the old man.

"How you all figure this lady's a holy woman?" Meza asks.

"Like I said. My neighbor's nephew's girlfriend saw her in action while out on a trading expedition. She described the whole thing in detail. Boy, I would've loved to see something like that with my own eyes, I tell you what."

"She saw her fighting a hellion?"

"That's what I'm saying. A whole horde of 'em!"

"Thought hellions rarely venture into this region. The proximity to sludgebrain territory and all that."

"That's right. We ain't had a big incident involving them in years. Only a few lone stragglers here and there. But we keep watch for hordes just the same. From the towers, you can see if any are approaching from miles out."

Carl points out the 20-foot tower built into the wall as they enter the… tribe? No, that's not it, either.

There isn't much to the "town", and what is there isn't much to look at. Half of the square is given away to a scraggly patch of dull green, the bit of land the people here toil over for what will only ever amount to a modest harvest.

And in the center of the square, a small blockhouse fortified with a combination of wood and rusted metal.

A church with a second lookout tower atop it stands out as the largest of the dozens of buildings surrounding the square. Though calling some of these wobbly shacks buildings may be a bit too generous.

Made of various combinations of warped wood, rusting scrap metal, and packed dirt brick, they barely look like they'd withstand the huff and puff of a hungry wolf. All major fortifications went into the wall and the blockhouse.

The good people of Hope mill about, doing whatever it is people in tiny places like this do. The smallest kids play in the dirt. A handful of people tend the garden. Another group tinkers with weapons on a porch.

The music of Queen drifts into the square from a small device perched in a window. "Don't Stop Me Now" has ended and the playlist is well into the next song.

Several faces and voices lift to join the refrain of "For meee"s.

Sebastian has never been prouder.

"But mostly," Carl continues on, "whoever's on tower duty sits around bored for a few hours until their replacement comes, unless it's sludgebrain season, of course. We see plenty of action then. But that's usually just once a year. It's the darnedest thing how hellions hordes been showing up all around these parts lately. This holy woman was sent to us at just the right time."

"Huh," Sebastian says. "That *is* the darnedest thing. And how close to this miraculous lady showing up did all the hellions start making an appearance? Asking for a friend."

As if summoned by Sebastian's voiced suspicions, the keening wail of an alarm shatters the calm of the square.

In unison, Sebastian and Meza draw their Devastators, brace the weapons against their shoulders, and pivot so that they're back to back. Their eyes scan the top of the wall, the open gate, the sky for the threat.

It's a reflex that comes as easy as breathing.

Because here's the thing about life after the fall of civilization: Everyone from the smallest child to the oldest man knows that there's no such thing as peace and safety. Even in those small, happy moments that almost feel like perfection, one's finger is never too far from the trigger of a reliable weapon.

And so it is that the second the alarm sounds, the good people of Hope drop whatever they're doing and prepare to face battle, and their probable deaths.

Weapons are snatched from holsters. Leaders call out commands. Children are swept indoors, and most likely into hidey-holes dug into the foundation of the homes.

Some men and women race to join the lookouts in the two towers. The more shooters at a higher vantage point the better. Others flock to the gate, pointing their blasters outward as those who'd been outside the wall race through the closing gap.

With a flick of his wrist, Sebastian activates his holo-interface and stabs at the bright red button at the bottom of the display. Though he can't see it happening, he knows HRM is drawing in her awning and shuttering her windows.

Firing starts from the tower near the gate. The monstrous creatures are already close.

"Watch the curios!" Sebastian cries, thinking of the set up he'd spent hours perfecting despite feeling less than one hundred-percent this morning. HRM is armored. The curios are not. "See, Meza. This is why I can't have nice things."

If the gunners manning the enormous rapid-fire Ravagers do their jobs like the rock stars Sebastian hopes they are, the hellions won't make it past the wall.

The problem is that when these monsters show up en

masse, they're like a force of nature. They don't let something as insignificant as heavy casualties or massive injuries slow them down. It's all or nothing with them. Headshots for all the hellions or the poor humans in their path are nothing but dinner.

"Move," Meza says. Sebastian doesn't have to be told she means the blockhouse in the center of the square. Best not to be standing out in the open if the hellions make it over—or through—the wall.

A few steps away, Carl fumbles with his blaster, drops it.

"Meza," Sebastian says, and nods toward the old man. They reconfigure themselves to put Carl between their backs.

"Shouldn't you be inside with the kids, Grandpa?"

"I been standing my ground against these things since before you were born! I was at the battle of—"

"Remember our deal? I believe everything you say you did if you spare me the trips down memory lane. Can you make it to the blockhouse?"

"'Course I can!"

Carl recovers his weapon and they're moving toward the center of the square. The structure cobbled together with wood and metal isn't much to look at, but it's better than nothing.

They're still precious yards away when writhing, black shadows fall over the square like giant locusts coming to chow down on some juicy crops.

Fun fact about walls, even impressive metal ones. They are significantly less useful when the monsters have wings.

And no, not all hellions can fly. There are as many types of these creatures as there are covers of Leonard Cohen's "Hallelujah". A great number of them are flightless. This just happens to be Hope's lucky day.

The screeching hellions crisscross over the sky like those

flying monkeys in one of the old movies Sebastian found while mining the streams for new music. Their numbers are small, for a horde, but that's like saying you have a small hole in your boat. You're sinking either way.

One of the grayish-brown creatures lands on a roof thirty yards away from Sebastian, its claws clang noisily against the metal. It leaps to the ground ahead of a spray of blaster fire. On its four spindly legs, it moves even more swiftly.

Sebastian fires Captain. The Devastator unleashes its fury, but the thing zigzags so fast the hot blue energy blasts can't pin it down. The hellion is twenty yards from Sebastian. Ten yards. Five.

Meza whips her Waster from her shoulder holster and fires past Sebastian. The monster drops, the shot catching it dead in the center of its forehead.

But she's so busy covering Sebastian's ass she doesn't see the brute charging toward them from her left. Sebastian swivels, pivoting Captain's barrel with him. Even as he moves, he knows he's not going to make it.

"Halt!" The commanding, feminine voice rises above the ruckus.

And then, weirdly, the hellion stops.

It's as if, mid-charge, the creature is struck by the urgent realization that it shouldn't be doing this and so plants its claws in the dirt for a tumbling halt. An ancient tires-against-road screeching sound would not have been out of place.

It lands mere inches from Meza and Sebastian's feet, glowers up at them. A vicious snarl rips from its throat.

Sebastian takes the shot.

Bull's-eye.

And sure, it's significantly easier to hit a target when it's standing still than when it's darting around like crazy, but still, he figures that makes him and Meza even.

Not that he's keeping score.

The most immediate danger dealt with, Sebastian scans his surroundings to find that all the other hellions—every single one of them—have come to a stop. With ears pricked, they look back toward the way they came. They seem almost confused.

From the towers and around the square, the people of Hope aim their blasters and make use of the unexpected advantage. Even still, the hellions don't move.

"Return to the hellish landscape from whence you were birthed!" the projected voice says.

The creatures flap their leathery wings and take flight, speeding back over the walls of Hope.

"With my mighty spirit powers, I command you! Begone!"

There's a whoosh of wind. A flash of light brighter than day, so bright Sebastian turns his face away.

And then, all is an unsettling quiet. No screeching monsters. No rattling of blaster fire. Just a bunch of bewildered folk staring at each other over the corpses of hellions and wondering what exactly just happened.

"The gate!" someone shouts from the tower. "Open the gate. Now!"

Whoever says it must have some clout, because the gate moves.

Smoke unfurls through the opening, and then music drifts inside.

Piano. Delicate and serene. But loud enough to drown out the Queen still playing in one of the windows. Sebastian recognizes the Bach composition. "Prelude in C Major."

"Brave people of Hope," a soothing, airy voice calls out. "Your fight is over. I have come."

A pair of white horses appear through the drifting smoke like heavenly apparitions. Behind them, they pull a hover-wagon. Also white, with pastel flowers painted on the sides.

Atop the wagon stands a woman in flowing white, her robes somehow immaculate when everyone and everything else is dingy and crusty from dirt. She seems to glow.

The gathering crowd gasps at the sight of her.

Sebastian squints, drifts forward for a better look. But from first glance, he knows he isn't seeing things. As much as he wishes he were.

"That ain't—" Meza says.

"That *is*." Sebastian shakes his head. "I'm an idiot. Shoulda known. I really shoulda known."

Because, of course, if there's a woman pulling off impossible miracles as a means to scam her way through town after town, who else could it be but—

"Chancy freakin' Freeman." Sebastian spits the name. Even just saying it leaves a bad taste in his mouth.

Sharp wit. Ambiguous ethnicity. Curves she's all but weaponized. Chancy freakin' Freeman isn't exactly beautiful, but she oozes confidence as if she were. Also, there's the plain fact that everything about her is captivating. She could charm the scales off a snake.

She is a woman who knows her power over others and takes full advantage, and she doesn't possess a single benevolent bone in her body.

Perfectly balanced as she's drawn into the center of the square, the woman in white smiles beatifically upon the dirty, upturned faces and allows herself to be adored.

She guides her wagon into a small loop using some complicated rigging that allows her to steer the horses from her position on the roof.

Presumably, she's gifting all her admirers with a good look at her in all her majesty. But as she draws to a stop, Sebastian doesn't miss the fact that she's pivoted her horses and wagon to face the open gate. Perfectly situated to make a quick exit, if needed.

She must activate the controls remotely because the wagon's parking gear pops out from the bottom and the engine cuts off. The current generators go silent as the wagon settles onto its legs.

"Who are you?" asks an awestruck woman with hard lines etched across her face.

"You may call me Sister," she says with such generosity that being able to call her anything must be a great gift. "Sister Sage Sojourner Mother Teresa King Chavez Mandela."

"Oh," Meza says.

"Wow," Sebastian agrees.

"How are you able to banish the hellions?" the same woman asks.

"Shall I tell you my story?"

"Yes," the crowd calls out. "Please." "You gotta!"

"Very well, my children."

Everyone has re-emerged from the buildings, down from the towers, and from across the square to gather all around the wagon for a better look.

"This oughta be good," Sebastian mutters. He scans the faces around him. There has to be at least one other person besides him and Meza who sees through this crap. But every one of these people is soaking it all in with wide, wondrous eyes.

"I was once a simple girl with simple wants." As *Sister Sage* speaks, she glides unhurriedly from one side of the wagon's roof to the other to address everyone equally. "I prayed only for food in my belly, my family safe, and, every once in a while, I even dared to dream of one day finding a simple, steady love."

She tucks her chin and looks at the crowd through her eyelashes, sweetly demure.

Sebastian snorts. A man standing in front of him throws an affronted look over his shoulder.

"I'm sorry," Sebastian says solemnly. The man lowers his hackles. That is, until Sebastian adds, "Sorry she wouldn't know love if it stabbed her in her withered black heart."

The man glares daggers at Sebastian, but he only moves away, eager to hear the rest of what will surely turn out to be a ridiculous tale.

"Until one tragic day that started out like any other, when the hellions fell upon my home. I lost everyone I knew and loved in an instant I will play over and over in my head for as long as I draw breath."

The crowd gasps.

"Pssh." Sebastian rolls his eyes. "Who hasn't? That's literally the story of everyone over the age of zero."

"I lost the will to live," she continues. "So I started walking. And walking and walking and walking. Suddenly, I found myself on the border of the Wasting West. And though I was merely a lone girl with no food, no allies, no possessions but the threadbare clothes on my back, I allowed my feet to carry me into that no man's land."

This earns her even deeper gasps. Awed murmurs spread through the crowd.

Sebastian can't listen a second longer. "Meza?"

She's just pulled her water canteen from her belt. "Yes, Sebastian?"

"It is our civic duty to discredit this charlatan before she takes advantage of these poor, innocent people."

"What happened to 'or we don't'?"

"What's that?"

"Don't Chancy deserve the chance to make her way in the world?"

At the moment, Chancy has her audience completely

enraptured as she spins an elaborate tale about the trials she supposedly endured in the Wasting West.

"I am shocked," Sebastian says, "that you would even suggest such a thing. I honestly thought you were better than that, Meza. How could we stand by and do nothing?"

Meza taps her chin. "Oh, I get it. Things are different when the swindler is someone who's swindled you. That tracks."

"She did not swindle me! She merely appealed to my big heart and immensely generous nature."

"And how long were you stranded in that town where she left you high and dry?"

"But I got Her Royal Majesty back! Why don't you start with that part of the story?"

The corners of Meza's mouth almost curl upwards, but as usual, she bites back her smile. She takes a swig from her canteen. "Don't know how you survived before I came along."

"Oh, whatever." Sebastian marches away. "Nobody's interested in your commentary. Just keep an eye out for your opening, *Honor*."

She glares at him. No one calls her by her first name. Sebastian only learned it after she lost a hand of poker.

"Excuse me," Sebastian says, parting the crowd as he moves toward the wagon. "Excuse me. Pardon me. Thank you."

Chancy's back is to him as he climbs the ladder attached to the wagon. She's so busy hamming it up for the crowd that she doesn't notice him until he's pulling himself onto the wagon's roof.

"So you see, I—" She falters for only a second as recognition flickers across her face, and then she turns back to her audience and finishes the tale. "I did not find death, though I felt it stalking me the entire time I endured that terrible place. I entered a girl, but I emerged a spiritually awakened woman with powers never before seen and a mission to do the impossible. To drive the hellions out of our world!"

A cheer rises up from the crowd.

She throws a dazzling smile at Sebastian. "As I live and breathe, is it *the* Sebastian Yun? I am truly blessed by the heavens to meet someone as highly esteemed as yourself, up close and personal. You are a much-needed force of positivity in this broken world."

"Cut the act, Chancy." Sebastian doesn't have the benefit of whatever device she's using to project her voice. He has to settle for talking really, really loud. "You had to know your ruse wouldn't last forever."

She places a palm against her chest, the very picture of innocence. She can't be that much older than him. A year. Maybe two.

Then again, she could be a hundred and ten. Chancy Freeman is the type to transform into whatever age is convenient for her in the moment. It's not very hard at all for poor fools to underestimate the depths of her deviousness.

"Why, Mr. Yun," she says. "I have absolutely no idea to what you are referring. I have never met you before a day in my life. Perhaps you have me mistaken for someone else. I'm told I have one of those faces."

She taps the data cuff on her wrist as she draws in close, smile as sweet as gentle rain.

"Listen." Her words are no longer projected over the square, and she ditches the soft and ephemeral quality of her voice. "Ruin this for me, honey bun, and I promise to make you regret it for a very long time."

"I'll more than ruin this for you," he replies, conversationally. "Every time I broadcast, I'm starting with an extremely thorough description of your lovely self and every bit of detail about this con you're pulling. I'll make you so famous you'll never be able to run another scam for the rest of your life."

Her smile is frozen on her face, but her eyes flash anger. "Unless?"

"Unless you tell me how you're doing this and hand over whatever it is you're using to do it."

She spins to once again face the people of the… parish? No. Too churchy. When she speaks, her voice is projected. "I'm sorry, everyone. This poor, poor young man is extremely disturbed and in dire need of my immediate private counsel."

The crowd looks at Sebastian, clicking their tongues with pity. He throws up his hands. Just yesterday, he was cool with all of them. A flash-in-the-pan celebrity strides into town and now his name is mud.

Who knew the public could be such a fickle mistress?

Moments later, Sebastian is sitting on a cushioned bench across from Chancy in her surprisingly spacious wagon. It looks like a rainbow suffered explosive diarrhea in here.

From the curtains shut tight over the windows to the blankets on the bed at the head of the wagon to the plush pillows tossed everywhere, the little wagon contains every color under the sun. The vibrant contrast to the bland brownness outside almost hurts Sebastian's eyes.

But the circulated air is as cool as ice water, a welcome relief from the heat of the day. Running an environmental control system requires a lot of power. She clearly spares no expense when it comes to her comfort.

From a compartment hidden beneath a cushion, she retrieves a small jug. After uncorking it, she pours a healthy portion of brown liquid into a tin mug, downs it in one swallow, then gives herself a refill. Only then does she half fill a second mug, which she offers Sebastian.

He rejects it with a wave of his hand.

She has the nerve to look offended. "What? You don't really think I'd poison you, do you?"

"You mean again?"

She rolls her eyes. "How long are you going to hold that against me? It obviously wasn't a lethal dose. Why would I ever wanna deprive the world of such a pretty face?"

"Your extremely accurate flattery will get you nowhere, flimflam woman. Tell me how you do it."

She tsks. "Who taught you to negotiate, Bazzy Bun? You didn't even give me the chance to make a counter offer. What if I were to give you half my take from this town? All you have to do is keep that fat mouth of yours shut for once in your life."

"Ain't interested."

"Fine. Forty percent of everything I've… acquired so far. I'd think twice before saying no. I've been at this for weeks. And I'm telling you. This is my best hustle yet. Towns will impoverish themselves for the services of a genuine exorcist. And before you say it, is it really my fault if folks out here are dumb enough to fall for anything?"

Why did those words sound so eerily familiar?

Sebastian must have heard them in a song or something.

He crosses his arms. "Has anyone ever told you that you are the worst human being ever?"

She grins. "Missed you, too, sweet cake. You know I live for our little tête-à-têtes, don't you?"

"Stop trying to distract me. It won't work."

"And I tune in to hear your show every single day. You, sir, have a gift. Your taste in music is truly divine."

"I mean, well, yeah. I am really good at what I do."

"It's more than that. You're a rare breed, Sebastian Yun. You make life interesting. How could I not think about you on a daily basis?"

"Oh, you're just being modest."

"I am a lady, after all."

"You're many things, Chancy freakin' Freeman. A lady ain't one of them."

She leaves her bench for his, sidles up real close. And in the coolness of the wagon, her warmth up against his isn't such a terrible thing.

"Dumpling," she says. "I'll be whatever you want me to be."

"You sure? I have a pretty good imagination."

"I'm game if you are. Let's say we can pick up where we left off last time, and maybe make up for lost time while we're at it?" She plucks at his collar, exposing more of his skin.

"Hard to say no to an offer like that. Especially coming from a girl like you."

"Then you'll mind your business, just this once, hmm?" Her finger follows the shape of his collarbone. "You go on your merry little way, pick the town to rendezvous in, and I'll make good on my offer."

He grabs her wrist, stops her exploring touch before it brushes the scars peeking out from beneath his shirt. "We both know you wouldn't show."

She exhales heavily, pulling her wrist free.

"You ain't making this easy, shug." She tugs at her white robes, tossing the layers until they look messy. "But I want you to remember that I tried to be more than reasonable here."

She runs her fingers through her short hair until it's disheveled and standing every which way.

Sebastian realizes what she's about to do seconds before she does it.

He springs away from her like she's just caught fire.

She screams bloody murder.

"Son of a—"

"Help!" she cries. "Help! He's a mad man!"

The back door of the wagon flies open.

"What's going on in here?"

"Nothing!" Sebastian says, both hands raised as if that alone would be enough to prove his innocence.

"Oh, thank heaven!" She throws herself out the door and into the arms of the big, burly bearded man who had wrenched it open.

"There, there, little lady." The bearded man gives Chancy's back a comforting pat while at the same time spearing Sebastian with a look that could freeze the sun. "Why don't you tell us exactly what happened?"

"Nothing happened!" Sebastian steps out of the wagon, hands still raised. What had been her worshipful audience has just that quickly transformed into a glowering mob. "Nothing except that I once again underestimated how conniving that snake in woman's clothing really is."

Chancy shudders with a thick, overdramatic sob.

"I—I think he was trying to kill me," she says, breathless. "I was so very frightened. I know how to fight hellions." She sniffles. "I didn't realize I was so helpless against real monsters." She adds a convincing quiver to her voice.

"Oh, come on!" Sebastian's eyes roll toward the sky.

Meza stands off from the crowd, unflappable as she watches the metaphorical torches and pitchforks come out. Her eyes flicker toward Chancy's wagon so quickly Sebastian might have missed it. But he catches her meaning.

"Look at you," the bearded man says to Chancy. "Young enough to be my daughter. What a brave little lady."

Mr. Beardy—who, by the way, looks like he eats iron nails for breakfast and wrestles ten-foot hellions on his downtime —gazes down at her with a nauseating softness in his eyes. Like she's the most delicate and precious thing in all of existence.

"And that makes me young enough to be your son." Sebastian slowly steps away from the wagon, drawing everyone's attention with him until all backs are to it, including Chancy's. "Where's my sympathy?"

"I knew I didn't like the looks of you the second you rolled into town," says a woman with a scar across her mouth.

Several people nod and chime in with their agreement.

Behind them all, Meza saunters toward the wagon. Sebastian forces his gaze away from her as she slips through the open back door.

"Really, Esther?" Sebastian says to scar lady. "The second I rolled into town you practically tried to rip my clothes off."

"Hey!" a tall man says. "Watch what you say about my wife."

"Wife? She didn't mention she was married. I wonder why…"

"You little punk—"

"String 'im up!"

Still tucked under the bearded man's protective arm, Chancy smirks.

"Whoa!" Sebastian says. "Whoa. Let's not get too hasty. It ain't my fault the ladies fall in love with my voice. Can you really blame them? Listen to this silky goodness.

"But more to the point, I know this charlatan. I know how easy it is to fall for her lies, and as much as she may have it coming, I did not try to hurt her. I was simply wasting my breath trying to convince her to come clean about this racket she's running. Shoulda known she ain't have it in her to do right."

Chancy buries her face in Mr. Beardy's shirt. "Why is he saying such awful things about me? I just wanna use my gift to help my fellow man."

"So nobody else finds it a mite bit suspicious that in the

region where hellion hordes are few and far between, they seem to follow her everywhere she turns up?"

"I go where my holy visions take me."

"Holy visions? More like you catch the scent of gullible marks."

"Oh, my!" She gasps, lays the back of her hand dramatically against her forehead. "What if this angry boy is correct? Perhaps I am the cause. My dear, sweet Lord, could it be that all this time these creatures been attracted to my immense spiritual power? If that's true, I should banish myself to the Wasting West where I can no longer pose a threat to anyone."

"Nonsense," the people of Hope cry. "That's poppycock!" "Please don't go, Sister!" "How can we convince you to stay, Sister?"

Nobody else seems to catch the greedy glint that sparkles in her eye. "Well—"

"Banishment sounds good to me," Sebastian says. "Find it?"

"Found it." Meza hangs out of Chancy's wagon, waving a clunky, cylindrical device the size of her forearm. "I think."

She steps the rest of the way from the door and cuts through the crowd, thoroughly engrossed in her examination of the device.

When Chancy's eyes fall on the gadget, they grow wide. A flash of panic she quickly covers. It's all the confirmation Sebastian needs.

"Poor, hurt Sebastian Yun," Chancy says. "Still trying to get back at me after our little run in back in North Dam. That's ancient history. You really oughta get over it."

"Ha!" Sebastian says. "So you do know me. That's one lie exposed, people. Makes you ponder what else she's fibbing about, don't it?"

Mr. Beardy looks down at Chancy, eyebrows furrowed. Perhaps not so certain about the brave little lady after all.

Though Sebastian's small victory is tempered by the knowledge that her admission of this truth is no slip of the tongue.

Her every word is a snare set for the unwitting. The only question is what trap is she laying out this time?

"Ain't sure what it is." Stopping at Sebastian's side, Meza turns the device over in her hands. It's crudely made, even by Midland standards. An unattractive tube of tech with exposed circuits and wires sticking out every which way.

Chancy shrugs out of the bearded man's arms, pointedly does not look toward the ugly device. "You young guys are great. Really. I love your enthusiasm, but I simply ain't a hitch-her-wagon type of girl."

"Never seen anything remotely like it—"

"But it ain't nothing to be bitter about, sugar." Chancy closes the distance between her and Sebastian. "We had a fun string of nights there, didn't we?"

"—so by process of elimination—" Meza's head snaps up. She looks from Chancy to Sebastian. From Sebastian to Chancy. "Wait! What? You and her?"

Chancy shifts toward Meza. "Don't worry, doll face. I'm through with him. You can have him all to yourself."

Meza freezes. Her mouth flaps open and closed a few times before she manages, "I don't—I ain't—me and him are not—will *never*—!"

Chancy makes a grab for the gadget.

Sebastian snatches it out of her reach. "Really, Meza? The idea upsets you so terribly?"

Lips pursed into a tight grimace, she shoves her fists in her pockets. Her gaze finds the ground and stays there. "Don't start with me, Sebastian."

"Trouble in paradise?" Chancy says with a chuckle.

Sebastian reaches for Tennille, the Waster at his hip. "You want trouble, honey bun?"

Throwing the ugly device into the air, he pulls his blaster and fires. Quick-draw style.

"Sebastian, no!" Meza shouts at the same time that Chancy yells, "Don't!"

But the blast is already blazing toward the device. Direct hit. A truly impressive shot.

Chancy's device clatters to the ground several feet away, in the shadow of the tower by the gate. Just beyond the now-even-uglier device and through the open gate, Sebastian's Itty-Bitty Carnaval de Mécanique Curios is still mostly standing at HRM's broad side.

"What were you so worried about?" Sebastian says, in a particularly fine mood, what from thwarting Chancy's scheme and seeing that his curios mostly survived the earlier onslaught of hellions. "Whatever that thing is, it looks good and dead to me."

The device jumps as if highly offended by Sebastian's assessment.

"You idiot," Chancy says.

The crowd shouts in alarm and takes several, big cautious steps back as the twisted, blast-burned device convulses violently. It spasms across the dirt, throwing off hissing sparks and kicking up little dust clouds.

Sebastian re-holsters Tennille and brandishes Captain instead. He aims the 18-inch barrel at the device.

"We about to run for our lives thanks to me, ain't we?"

Meza sighs, pulling out her own Devastator. "Yes. Again."

"What exactly does that thing do, Chanc—?"

The space beside Sebastian is empty but for a plume of dust. Chancy is already climbing into the driver's box of her wagon.

"You really are the worst, Chancy freakin' Freeman!" Sebastian shouts after her.

"I'll miss you, too, love muffin!" She has the nerve to blow a kiss before flicking the reins and speeding through the gates, passing right over her malfunctioning gadget in her hurry to abandon the—community?

Too wishy-washy.

Sebastian would love nothing more than to drag her back and force her to face whatever's about to happen next, but it's times like these that knowing one's priorities are a matter of life and death.

And when the convulsing cylinder coughs up a narrow sliver of light, priorities become crystal clear.

Sebastian has never seen this type of thing with his own eyes, that doesn't mean he can't recognize what's happening.

The razor thin slice of light zigs across the empty space above the device. It's small. The length of a man's boot. But big or small, a crack in the very fabric that makes up the world is still a crack in the very fabric that makes up the world.

"A fissure," Meza breathes, disbelieving. "Crazy chick found a way to open fissures into the hellions' dimension on demand."

These days, fissures are a naturally occurring part of this paradise called Earth, and as unpredictable as twisters. Of course, it wasn't always so.

Once upon a time, a clever scientist looked around at the death and mayhem that had befallen humanity and got it into his head to do something about it. But this world was obviously screwed, so the obvious solution obviously was to find a place where mankind could pop a squat in peace for the rest of eternity. Obviously.

Like regrettable exes and haircuts, everyone could just move on and pretend that other place was never a thing.

But you know how it is, working under pressure. Plus, scientific funding wasn't what it used to be, what with the fall of civilization and all that jazz.

So the equipment wasn't exactly state-of-the art and there was an extremely frustrating understaffing problem. Those hard-to-find, qualified prospects that the scientist managed to recruit had this terribly unprofessional habit of not surviving the hellish landscape that was the world.

Long story short, the scientist succeeded in finding another world, but while he was at it, did a mighty fine job of breaking the barrier between dimensions. And that other world just happened to be filled with ravenous, bloodthirsty monsters.

Once they found their way into this classy joint, these doubtful guests were not inclined to leave.

And humanity had one more thing out there trying to kill them. Just what they needed.

Thanks, science.

Fissures pop up less frequently now than when the world first broke, but that doesn't mean anyone wants to be within spitting distance when one decides to burst open.

And Sebastian definitely doesn't want to be trapped inside the walls of this commune... No, that word is too peace, love, and happiness-y... when that glowing fissure starts spewing out hellions. Whatever way Chancy had of sucking the hellions back into their world isn't abundantly obvious, and she did not think to toss them a user's manual before leaving everyone to die.

The image of fish in a barrel comes to mind. Hidey-holes, defensive towers, and a ramshackle blockhouse won't be enough to withstand the type of trouble sure to come through that fissure.

"Run!" Sebastian shouts. "Everybody clear out!"

As a general rule, people who live to see the next day in a grim, post-apocalyptic world don't have to be told "run" twice.

"To the bus!" Meza hollers.

"What?" Sebastian says. "I mean, yeah. To the bus! But nobody touches my hologram action figure collection. They're antiques!"

It'll be tight, but since this is not a town, but a… something Sebastian couldn't quite find the name for at the moment, everyone could probably squeeze in. Better to speed away and start over somewhere else than to fight for this pile of twigs and rust against impossible odds.

Sebastian and Meza lead the race for the gate, eyes and Devastators trained on the fissure. Now four times longer than it was only moments ago, it jerks through the air as if tied to the spastic cylinder by a taut string.

They just need a few more seconds to get past it. Sebastian prays desperately. Just a few tiny, measly seconds. *Please.*

Sebastian has often wondered how the hellions know to come through the fissure.

Is there a smell that broadcasts "Fresh meat this-a-way"? Does it take time for hellions to find the fissures over on their side? Are they sitting around in their world, twiddling their claws and waiting patiently for an opening into the magical world of scrumptious, slow-moving snacks, please and thank you very much?

Or how often do these things open but there are no monsters waiting on the other side?

It would be nice if on the other side of this fissure it's nothing but some barren landscape that even monsters avoid.

Really, really nice.

The device hiccups and the fissure grows as long as the width of the gate. They would have to jump over it to get out.

They can make it.

Something thin and black and spindly pokes through the fissure.

It's just one little thing. They can still make it.

Suddenly, dozens more explode through the gap. They look like thin, black fingers. Or maybe colossal spider legs. Some short, some tall as a person. Whatever they are, they haven't fully emerged through the gap yet, but these limbs reach and claw as if they can sense all the nummy treats just out of their grasp.

Sebastian pulls to a halt and stops way too close to the brimming fissure for comfort. Leveling Captain, he lets loose a spray of blaster fire. Other weapons fire beside him.

The whole town takes up a cry of "Fall back! Fall back!" Children are once again swept indoors and, Sebastian assumes, into their hidey holes.

For what it's worth.

A number of townspeople hold the line with Sebastian and Meza, even as they move back together and out of range of those reaching limbs.

Others fly toward the towers. If there was ever a time to let loose with the Ravagers, this would definitely be it.

Some of the black spindly things recoil and retreat from the sting of blaster fire, but some push forward. Then, finally, the first few crawl completely through the light. They're ugly enough to make Sebastian lose his lunch.

Too many legs.

They have way too many legs. Long and knobby, those legs raise slimy, lumpy round bodies high off the ground.

Boogers.

These particular hellions look like giant boogers on sticks.

The globulous bodies split open across the middle to reveal mouths full of needle-sharp teeth.

Terrifying giant boogers on sticks.

One of them rears up, flailing its front limbs wildly, almost doubling its height.

Sebastian fires at it, but Captain doesn't respond. The charge is dead.

As if sensing Sebastian's failed attempt on its life, the hellion turns all of its beady eyes on him. It dives into an attack.

Dropping Captain, Sebastian whips out Tennille. He catches the hellion square between all four eyes. But momentum keeps the now corpse barreling forward.

The slimy ball slams into him, sends him sprawling onto his back and coughing on dust. The monster's massive weight pins him in place.

It is not a pleasant experience.

With blaster fire focused on the immediate threat of the marching monsters, more and more terrifying giant boogers on sticks pull themselves through the glowing crack as if climbing out from the belly of hell.

Sebastian's fall seems to send an alert to the other creatures. *Easy prey, easy prey, easy prey.* Several of them, too many of them, zero in on him. And they look mighty hungry as they lunge. Teeth gnashing. Eyes glinting.

All the townsfolk are too busy with their own messes to bother with getting Sebastian out of his.

Well, Sebastian always knew he would die young, though he never quite pictured going out like this. At least he won't have to worry about suffering through any more of Carl's boring "back in my day" lectures.

Meza appears, planting herself between Sebastian and the oncoming hellions. She's inhumanly calm. The way she takes aim and fires is almost matter of fact.

"Any time you want to join in would be good, Sebastian."

"Oh, sorry. Let me just get this enormous, dead monster off of me all by myself."

"Excuses."

A shrill siren rings out from the tower.

"What now?" Sebastian asks.

"Everyone's turning tail. Making for the blockhouse. We need to clear out. Now."

Sure enough, the good people of Hope are cutting and running. The sun glints off the enormous blasters in the tower near the gate. They're pointed directly at the growing horde of hellions.

One problem with that.

"They're about to fire the Ravagers!" Sebastian pushes against the slick monster corpse pinning him down. "Help me get this off!"

Sebastian's hands sink into the dead hellion's disturbingly thick coating of slime, but it's not until Meza crouches down to help that the thing budges.

The Ravager fire starts even as Sebastian squirms out from beneath the corpse. Either someone has a happy trigger finger, or his and Meza's lives are expendable in the grand scheme of things.

"Must not be fans of the show." Sebastian scoops up his weapons and runs like the wind.

The heat of blaster fire whizzes by uncomfortably close as he and Meza dash toward the blockhouse. The people who make it there first quickly take up positions with their weapons aimed through the narrow blaster loops. More Ravagers are pointed at the horde from the church tower.

Together, Sebastian and Meza run along the perimeter, clear of any blaster fire sure to come down the center of the square.

Space is tight in the blockhouse. Sebastian leans against one of the rough, wood beams in the center holding the whole thing up. His heart pounds as rapidly as all the blaster fire rattling off from the Ravagers. A walkie-talkie screeches.

"Hold your fire as long as the Ravagers keep the hellions

contained," a grizzled woman at the first blaster loop says. "Save your charges for when we really need 'em."

She carries an air of unquestioned authority. Plus, she has an eye patch. Grizzled people with eye patches are automatically in charge. Thems the rules.

"Gotta get out of here," Meza says. "Before something even worse comes through that fissure."

"Tell me something I don't know." Sebastian switches out the dead charge of his Devastator for a fresh one strapped at the base of his handguard. He pumps the weapon once to connect the new charge and Captain comes alive with an electric whine.

"It closed!" a voice says over the crackling walkie-talkie. "The fissure just closed all on its own."

"Maybe it's over?" someone in the blockhouse asks.

Sebastian shoves his way to a blaster loop for a look out into the square. He's always wondered why they're called "loops". They don't loop at all. They're narrow, crisscrossing slits that allow blasters a wide range of movement without exposing the shooter. If anything, they should be called blaster crosses.

Peering through the poorly named loop, Sebastian confirms that, sure enough, the glowing rip between dimensions is gone. From the towers, the Ravagers are doing their job and doing it well. The booger monsters have thinned to only a few, then it's just one, then the blaster fire dies.

In the new quiet, Freddy Mercury wails about finding love.

No one celebrates the victory. The air itself seems to be holding its breath.

"Wanna make another run for it?" Sebastian hasn't finished whispering the question—because in the unsettled silence, whispering feels like the only option—when the cylindrical device hops and hiccups and a fissure opens again. This one is small, but a spindly black limb pokes through.

The device hiccups again and the fissure snaps shut, slicing the limb clean off.

"Too unpredictable." Meza, squeezed close to peer through the blaster loop below him, voices what Sebastian was thinking about the fissures even as he'd asked the question. "Didn't make it the first try. Started closer to the gate that time."

"Right now, that doo-hickey is wounded," Sebastian says. "These are like its death throes. We need to put it out of its misery."

"You're a poet," Meza says.

"I try."

Carl is suddenly at their right. "If more of them suckers come out, ain't nobody getting close to that thing."

"Well, not with that attitude, Negative Nancy," Sebastian says. "I propose we shoot at it a bunch more. Use the Ravagers. Let's make sure that thing's really destroyed this time."

"Sounds good to me," says the woman with the eye patch. She holds her walkie to her mouth. "Fire on the device. Quick, before more—"

"Too late," Sebastian says.

The device seems to throw up. But instead of wet chunks, it spews the biggest fissure yet. The Ravagers let loose, but the blasts are swallowed by the gaping, fizzling crack in the world.

And in response to this generous offering, an enormous black column shoots out from the fissure.

It's as thick as a tree trunk and Sebastian waits for it to stop rising up, but it just keeps coming. And coming. And coming.

"First round were the babies," Meza says. "Reckon we done pissed off the mother."

"The nerve of us," Sebastian says. "Not letting her precious darlings chomp on our flesh."

The Ravagers fire away at it. The giant limb jerks from the impacts and then swings wildly toward the source of its pain. It collides into the tower on the first try. The tower never stood a chance.

With the painful sound of metal rending from metal, the 20-foot tower tears away from the attached structure. The gunners at the Ravagers scream and shout as it crashes down.

The fall isn't clean like a toppled tree. As it collapses, the former tower breaks and bows, almost in slow motion, like an old man begrudgingly taking a knee.

What was once a gloriously rusting column pointed to the sky is reduced to a sharp and tangled heap of twisted metal beams and sheeting filling an ugly gash in the no-longer-quite-as-protective wall.

And then, two more humongous knobby limbs explode from the fissure.

"So," Sebastian says. "It's been nice knowing you, Meza. If you got any declarations of love you been saving for our final seconds on this Earth, now would be the time for it."

"'Love' would not be my four-letter word of choice."

"Aw."

The woman with the eye patch curses. "Open fire! Open fire!"

A pair of townsfolk, Jo and Hope #1, Sebastian realizes, push him and Meza out of the way, replacing them at the blaster loop.

"Can't let that thing through," Meza says to Sebastian.

"I don't think we got much choice in the matter."

Even with the second tower firing away and all the

blasters of Hope combined, there's no way they're taking out something of that size.

An idea comes to him, but even he thinks it's crazy. Or maybe it's inspired. Meza would think it's ridiculously stupid.

Sebastian tries to get another look at the fissure, but with all the blaster loops occupied, his view is limited. He moves toward the blockhouse's side door.

Meza's on his heels. "Where you going?"

Nobody stops them from leaving. Maybe everyone figures Sebastian and Meza have the right to decide whether to die inside the blockhouse or out. Or maybe they're a little distracted at the moment. Could be either/or.

Sebastian squats down beside the blockhouse and squints at the fissure. It's parallel to the ground. Perhaps because of the massive hellion coming through, the cylindrical device isn't bouncing around anymore. It appears to be pinned in place.

"Hey," he says to Meza, "that space under the fissure. Think it's wide enough for a person to crawl under it?"

Meza's eyes narrow to thin slits. Yep, she's definitely leaning toward ridiculously stupid. "You'd never make it."

"Sure, I can. I just need a little cover is all." He points toward the wreckage of the fallen tower. "And now that we got us a way past these walls, I know how to get some. You with me?"

She lets out a slow breath, heavy with every one of her doubts. "Of course."

Skirting the perimeter, they avoid the lines of fire from the second tower and blockhouse as they hurry toward the collapsed tower and the gash in the wall.

The giant, thrashing limbs aren't any less terrifying up close. Not one bit. Especially when another limb bursts through. Bent at their knobby joints, the limbs brace against the ground the way a person would if trying to pull themselves out of a hole.

Sebastian inspects the rubble that used to be a tower. It's higher than it looked from the blockhouse.

Getting out will require some careful climbing over jagged, twisted metal and jutting, splintered wood. It means holstering his blaster.

He swallows and reminds himself that even a Devastator as awesome as Captain won't do a lick of good against the hellion trying to come through the fissure.

Surprisingly, the thought doesn't comfort him all that much.

"This way." Meza jumps onto the rubble. She scrabbles up and over the wreckage like it's as simple as hopping from stone to stone to get across a little stream.

Sebastian isn't quite as graceful, but he follows her sure steps.

"I swear she ain't human," he mutters, watching her go.

The wreckage creaks, and then crumbles beneath his feet. His heart leaps into his throat as he throws himself forward.

His hands catch something. Pain stings his palm. He hangs from a chunk of metal that juts out at an odd angle. Blood trickles down his arm. The cut must be pretty deep. But, hey, points for not tumbling to his death.

Glimpsing a potential foothold that he *just* might be able to make, Sebastian swings his legs forward. His toes find purchase on the less than certain surface. Then he's stuck. Toes ahead of him, fingers clinging to the chunk of metal above him. All his weight wants to pull him back, down into the newly formed pit of death and pointy things waiting to catch him.

"Careful!" Meza chides, doubling back.

"Really? But I thought now would be the perfect time to take up bull riding."

"Why would you ride a cow?" She reaches out, grabs a fistful of his shirt, and pulls. Sebastian lets go of the chunk of metal and collapses forward on a small, stable-ish platform created from a sizable width of rusted sheeting.

"Bull riding, not cow," he says between giant gulps of air. Meza helps him use a jagged piece of metal to tear an uneven strip off the bottom of his shirt. "In ye olde olden days, people used to climb on top of a huge angry animal with giant horns just to get thrown off, and then hope to get out of the way before it stomped or gorged them to death."

A screeching cry rings out. Behind them, the enormous body of the mama booger monster has emerged, screaming face first. The thing is just as ugly as the smaller hellions, but its teeth are the size of Sebastian.

The Ravager fire concentrates on the giant hellion's face and it retreats back. But no way is that the end of it.

Meza tightens the knot, securing the makeshift bandage around Sebastian's wounded hand and he picks himself up. "No time for a breather."

"Bull riding ain't a real thing," Meza says before turning to lead the way again.

"I'll show you old vids."

"Why would anybody do that?"

"For fun."

"Like a fun way to die?"

"I don't reckon the point was to die. Just to feel like you were about to." He watches her step delicately but quickly around a twisted tangle of metal before following.

"But not for real."

"For realsies."

"Old Worlders went out of their way to feel like they were about to die?"

Her words are nearly drowned out by another shriek from Mama Booger.

"I know," Sebastian says. "They would've loved it here."

"They'd get themselves killed here."

Finally, they come to a spot that lets them climb down outside the wall.

The handful of people who'd been at the top of the fallen tower have already begun to pull themselves together. A woman helps an injured man get clear of the rubble. A pair of guys only a little older than Sebastian work to right a Ravager, despite the blood running down their faces and arms. They must be hoping to drag it to the gate so they can continue the fight.

"Steer clear of the gate!" Sebastian calls out before he and Meza dart around the fallen tower to reach Her Royal Majesty.

Meza skids to a sudden stop and Sebastian collides into her.

"My curios!" Sebastian cries.

The Itty-Bitty Carnaval de Mécanique Curios has been decimated. Tables are capsized. All those innocent, little mechanical animals are in pieces, scattered around in the dirt.

The pair of hellions Sebastian and Meza have stumbled upon must've slipped out the gate earlier, and now they're trampling all over Sebastian's pride and joy.

Oh, and they're insanely close.

They look up, spot the two humans. With screeches that brandish rows of sharp teeth, the booger monsters charge.

Sebastian pulls Tennille at the same time that Meza pulls her own Waster, sadly unnamed.

In unison, they fire.

This time, Sebastian knows to dive out of the way as the lifeless bodies continue to fall forward.

The sight of the tiny dog shattered into even tinier pieces

is enough to break Sebastian's heart. He scoops up the metal bits. "You were too young, my friend."

"Mourn your toys later!" Meza is already flying through the tour bus' back door.

"You ain't got no heart." He races up the aisle behind her.

With the blast shields over the windows, the interior of the bus is pitch black but for the glow of Meza's holo-interface as she starts the engine from her data cuff before sliding behind the wheel.

As Sebastian dives into the passenger seat, the metal shutters pull back from the front window, letting in a flood of blinding daylight. There's the familiar little clang of the parking gear receding into the undercarriage and the shuttering breath of HRM's current generators cutting on.

Sebastian grips the dashboard to steady himself as Meza puts the bus in reverse and then yanks on the steering wheel. Moments later, they're lined up to face Hope's gate with several bus lengths between them. The enormous monster is seconds away from bursting fully into this world.

So far, the people of Hope have kept it from fully emerging, but even more legs have appeared. It seems to be using its own limbs as a shield. It's only a matter of time.

Sebastian deposits the pieces of the mechanical dog in one of the compartments of the front console. "Remind me. This was my idea?"

"Yup." Meza floors it.

The armored tour bus crashes through the open gate and a good chunk of the wall like it's nothing. It's the impact of colliding into the hellion's limbs that makes Sebastian glad he'd remembered to strap on the seat belt.

The limbs batter HRM.

"Hang in there, girl," Sebastian says, patting the dashboard. "Show this thing why you're the queen of the road."

Then, he slides the passenger side door open and takes that leap of faith.

Landing in the dust, he immediately crouches low. The giant, spindly legs swing at the bus. They're powerful, but clunky and awkward. Even if Mama Booger were aware of him, Sebastian doubts it would have the coordination to pluck him away from the side of the bus.

HRM shakes from the hellion's pummeling, and it occurs to Sebastian that it might not be impossible for the hellion to knock the bus over and crush Sebastian beneath it.

No reason to drag this out.

Captain drawn, Sebastian shimmies beneath the flailing monster limbs, beneath the glowing fissure as Mama Booger's face re-emerges through it. He thought the baby booger smelled bad when he was pinned beneath it. This stench is ten times worse.

He makes the mistake of opening his mouth for a breath and chokes on the dust thick in the air. It feels like he's been shimmying in the dirt forever when he finally reaches the damned device causing all this trouble. He takes aim.

"Why didn't I do this the first time?" Sebastian shouts, and he lets loose a hailstorm of blaster fire on the ugly cylinder.

This time, the device really will be good and dead.

The brightness of the fissure winks out, cutting off the humongous, half-emerged hellion. Then there's nothing but severed chunks of Mama Booger above him. And gravity. Let's not forget about gravity.

Sebastian tucks Captain against himself and rolls like the wind as giant monster limbs and half of a slimy monster body come crashing down around him.

After everything has settled, Meza finds Sebastian on his back among the pools of noxious blood, severed monster bits, and globs of quivering slime.

"Settlement!" Sebastian says when she's standing over him. "That's the word I was looking for. This is a settlement."

Sebastian takes Meza's offered hand, pulls himself to standing. He wonders if it would be more accurate to say this place *was* a settlement. There hadn't been much to this place before, now there's even less.

A tower down, the gate demolished, huge chunks of wall destroyed. Plus, when the hellion's humongous limbs came crashing down, they took out a couple of buildings.

The people of the settlement shuffle into the square and take in the damage. No jaws hang slack from shock. No hands fly to cover mouths in dismay. No tears stain cheeks with marks of devastation.

For the grim, glaze-eyed denizens of Hope, there is only the overwhelming inevitability of it all. Of knowing that what they build will again fall. That they will try to make themselves, their loved-ones safe, but there is no real protection from the monsters. That everyone they know will one day be destroyed by this savage world.

Somehow, Sebastian's block of Queen music is still streaming from that same window. No one else seems to appreciate that "Another One Bites the Dust" is playing.

Someone starts crying.

Sebastian flicks his wrist and his data cuff's holo-interface pops up. Turning on his mic, he broadcasts.

"Congrats, good people of Hope." Cutting off the music, his voice rings out across the square. "You have just survived some crazy shit. I, for one, was so sure it was a wrap for all of us. But we made it through. And I know three ladies who have something to say about that."

It's not his favorite song by Destiny's Child, but whenever and wherever he blasts "Survivor", it's like the sun breaking through a sky clogged with gray.

When he first discovered the song and started playing it

on his show, he wouldn't have guessed that a song about a pop group hemorrhaging members would become THE anthem for this era. But music is what people make of it.

By the time the song gets to the chorus, the people of Hope—from cranky, old Carl to the ten-year-old ringleader — join in to scream that they are survivors.

These dusty settlements, both big and small and somewhere in between, are all the same. When he was a kid, Sebastian thought grim and miserable were the only variety Midlanders came in. People were so busy surviving to the next day that even a simple smile was a luxury few could afford.

But as he watches the tiny, broke-down settlement of Hope celebrate, Sebastian thinks, *This.*

This is more like it.

Sure, the damage to the wall will need to be seen to immediately, and there's the clean up and tending to injuries. But for now—just this fleeting moment—there's laughter and singing and dancing because they have made it through another day of this terrible, messed up planet throwing the worst it's got at them.

A smile stretches across Sebastian's lips.

He catches Meza watching him.

"What?" he asks, still smiling.

She shrugs and walks away.

The clean up begins immediately. Sebastian pulls HRM out and parks it in front of the wide gap where the gate and some adjoining stretches of wall used to be. But the people of Hope work fast using scraps they'd stored away to replace the wall and rebuild the gate, because they have to, because that's how they survive.

The next day, Sebastian and Meza get a late start out. There had been a lot to do in Hope last night and Meza wanted to give Her Royal Majesty a thorough once over.

When Sebastian climbs into the bus and settles in behind the wheel, Meza is already in the passenger seat Sebastian had installed for her. She dozes with her feet kicked up on the dashboard and her arms crossed beneath the jacket she's pulled over herself.

Sebastian turns the engine over and a smooth, barely discernible vibration rumbles through HRM as she comes to life. A small motion on the dashboard catches Sebastian's attention.

The little mechanical dog chases its tail. It doesn't move as smoothly as it used to and it's clear where it was broken and put back together, but it lives again. And it's plugged directly into the tour bus' power.

He grins at Meza, even though she can't see it. "Ya big softy."

"Bite me," she mutters without opening her eyes.

"Love you, too, honey bun," he says in his best imitation of a certain female charlatan who shall remain nameless.

She doesn't dignify that with a response, so he talks to the mechanical dog instead.

"I'm calling you Shizzo." Sebastian gives the pooch a pat on its tiny, little head. "Welcome to the road."

WHAT'S NEXT? POST-APOCALYPTIC DJ: BOOK 1!

GRAB THE NEXT BOOK NOW AT
WWW.KCCORDELL.COM/BOOKS

Here's your sneak peak at Sebastian and Meza's next adventure: ***So Your Biggest Fan is a Body Snatcher (Post-Apocalyptic DJ: Book 1)***

"What the hell is wrong with you, Sebastian?" Meza grumbles over the roaring engine, pounding hooves, and yelling townsfolk. Sizzling blaster fire glows against the rapidly dimming sky.

"They started it!" Sebastian Yun puts pedal to the metal for all it's worth, but the mob screaming for his blood does an admirable job of keeping up despite the disparity in transportation modes.

In theory, horses should not be able to outpace a hover vehicle. But Her Royal Majesty, Sebastian's completely decked-out double-decker bus, is big and heavy. She was rebuilt to withstand monster assaults, not to win races.

Besides, it's not as if the parts Sebastian salvaged and pieced together to get HRM up and running were in the best condition to start with. Push the bus too hard and any of the many ancient parts keeping her going might just up and scream, "Screw this shit!" and depart for hoverbus-parts heaven.

Thus, he doesn't "put pedal to the metal for all it's worth" so much as put pedal to the metal as much as he dares while banking on the mob's horses tiring out very soon and quickly falling behind.

Meza pins him with a glare. It's almost as if she doubts his claim that this is all the townsfolk's fault.

"I did it for the children!" he says. "You know how kids are forced to live in them sorts of places? And you expected me to sit there and do nothing about that level of neglect? I am sorry, Meza, but that just ain't how I'm built."

"Right." With a roll of her eyes, Meza lowers the window. The clamor of the mob grows even louder.

The whooshing wind buffets against her halo of dark, textured hair as she props herself partly through the open passenger window. She grips the frame to steady herself with one hand while the other points her NX-84 Waster toward the back of HRM, where the horde of angry men and women on horseback ride like hell to keep up.

Face as placid as the moon, she fires a few shots. Warnings, that's all. A little something to make it clear that if the mob doesn't back down, she and Sebastian will defend themselves.

The message fails to land.

Return blasts light up the barren, darkening landscape in sporadic flashes. The armored bus shakes from the impact of a larger weapon but otherwise keeps on trucking.

Pun intended.

Fortunately, riding horseback and shooting accurately go together like Black Sabbath and tea parties. The sizzling blasts sail harmlessly past Meza. Hanging out the window with her own weapon drawn and lit by the blazing flashes, she looks like some kind of badass road warrior goddess.

Only a year younger than Sebastian, Meza is seventeen with a petite frame that borders on pixie. Not that he'd ever use that word to describe her. There's nothing sprite-like about her. For one thing, a cute little sprite sidekick would know how to have fun from time to time. In the handful of months they've known each other, Sebastian has yet to see her smile.

"I know you don't much like kids and all," he says, "but even you musta felt at least a little teeny, tiny ounce of pity for them."

"They were perfectly fine." She slips back into her seat and raises the passenger-side window.

"Perfectly—" He sputters, unable to believe that she would utter such flippant and callous words after witnessing that severely depraved situation with her own two peepers. He pushes unruly strands of black hair out of his eyes. Takes a breath. Prays for patience. "Meza. They ain't never heard any NWA ever. No Bone Thugs or Snoop. No Tupac!"

"Just couldn't help yourself."

"That's only West Coast '90s rap!" Sebastian says, to emphasize his point.

"It's called impulse control," she says, to reiterate hers.

He flicks his wrist to activate his data cuff. A round holo-interface pops up. Stabbing at a series of icons pulls up the feed from the camera embedded in the back of the bus. Cameras are not an easy get in the scavenging game, but at times like these, Sebastian is really glad he'd gone through the trouble.

The mob is still right on HRM's tail. They're a frantic knot of wild-eyed, frothing horses, angry-faced, shouting humans, and colorfully strobing blaster fire. All of it wrapped in an enormous dust cloud.

"They cannot still be keeping up," Sebastian says despite all evidence to the contrary. "What're they feeding them horses? Other horses? The hatred from the blackest parts of their shriveled hearts?"

"They're motivated. Far as they're concerned, you done doomed them all."

"'Cuz they heard a little music? Do they really not know how ridiculous they are?"

"More than that to them, and you know it."

"Barf! Anti-Techers. Literally the worst people in the Midlands. And, yes, that includes bandits and them idiots in the Congregation of Hope."

Although, to be fair, the average Midlander isn't overly trusting of tech. For some reason, computery stuff being the catalyst in the downfall of humanity doesn't sit well with a lot of people, even all these generations later. Go figure. As a result, most folks hadn't heard much Old World music before Sebastian started broadcasting a radio show that introduced all who would listen to delights from centuries long past. But this situation is different. These people are different.

"Ain't your place to judge what they believe," Meza says. "Just like it ain't your place to blast 'Hail Mary' at top volume from every corner of their town."

"Heh. Classic."

"Ain't laughing."

"What's new?" Sebastian asks. "Come on, even you gotta admit that was epic. Wish I coulda been inside their walls to see the look on that jerk of a town leader's face. She already looked like a professional salt sucker. Bet her whole face mighta caved in on itself."

"And that was worth all of this?" She waves a hand toward her window. Flashes of blue blaster fire brighten the dimming landscape.

"Don't you worry. They ain't catching us."

"Still leaves us on the road at night."

"Right… That."

"Right. That."

Admittedly, they are quickly approaching the wrong side of dusk, and the sky grows darker every second.

The evening hours are for shuttering windows and doors against all the things that go bump in the night. Not racing down the road attracting the attention of said night things with a bunch of noise and flashing lights.

Everybody knows this.

Everybody but the nutjobs riding furiously behind HRM.

Anti-Techers really are the worst.

"I did it for the fans!" Sebastian says. "You know I'd march into death itself for my adoring public."

"Ain't nobody in that town knew who you were."

He tosses her a lopsided grin. "They do now."

"Will you look so pleased when you're a corpse?"

Sebastian thinks about it for a few seconds. Really pictures it. "I genuinely hope so."

"For once can't you—"

"What? Be less awesome? I reckon that's like trying to contain a force of nature. Might as well ask the sun to stop shining."

She watches him, her lips drawn in a disapproving line.

His grin widens.

"Just drive."

So Your Biggest Fan is a Body Snatcher (Post-Apocalyptic DJ: Book 1)

READ IT TODAY!
www.kccordell.com/books

So Your Biggest Fan is a Body Snatcher (Post-Apocalyptic DJ: Book 1)

THE STORY BEHIND THE STORY

I'll level with you.

I did not expect that *So You Survived the End of the World* would be the book that I'd launch my publishing career with.

Before switching focus to what would become the Post-Apocalyptic DJ series, I'd been working on a series of novellas about four sisters who were adjusting to their lives as famous superheroes. I wrote three of those books and reached a stopping point on the fourth that I just couldn't get past.

Which was fine. That sometimes happens. Usually I just switch to another project and wait for my subconscious to tell me when it's figured out whatever problem needs to be fixed.

I had a bunch of stories I could have switched back to, but for whatever reason, that crazy one about a music-loving guy trying to live his best life in a post-apocalyptic wasteland called to me.

And it had been waiting for its moment to shine for a while.

Flashback to 2011. Or was it 2010?

Anyway, there I was. In the kitchen. Making lunch. When suddenly, a phrase popped into my head from out of nowhere.

So you survived the end of the world.

"Well," I said to myself. "That sounds like a title..."

It would have been irresponsible not to figure out what story belonged to it.

And, naturally, that story turned out to be about a music lover who has decided to share his passion despite living after the fall of civilization.

Clearly, it had to be post-apoc. I mean, it's right there in the title. Pretty low hanging fruit IMHO. But the music part, that was all me. What with me being super obsessed with music and taking joy in ~~forcing it upon~~ sharing it with the people around me. Bazzy is basically living my dream life. You know, the constantly-running-from-killer-monsters thing aside.

Once the story revealed itself to me, I became obsessed.

Every chance I got, I was writing away in my notebook as ideas tumbled out of my imagination faster, it seemed, than my pen could capture them. On the bus to work. Stopping for lunch at a sandwich place. During slow drags at the Borders bookstore (RIP) where I worked back then. Some of my original notes were scribbled on receipt paper that I fed out of the register during lulls between customers.

Soon I had pages and pages of dialogue and snippets of story and even a rough map of the wastelands. I envisioned it as a webcomic so I also had character sketches. And then I had a script. Then several scripts.

This fun-loving post-apocalyptic DJ, his grumpy traveling companion, and his shady nemesis came to life pretty much fully formed on the page. Although, I didn't have their names completely figured out yet... Sebastian Yun was originally Eric Yun. Chancy Freeman was originally Sean Freeman.

Honor Meza was originally Alice Meza. But I was halfway there at least. Not bad, younger me!

Somewhere after I had two and half webcomic scripts drafted, I realized that single-handedly creating a webcomic would require a TON of drawing, so I put it off. I figured I'd get around to climbing that artistic hill eventually...

Welp, nearly ten years passed with me meaning to get around to all that drawing.

While the webcomic didn't happen, the project was never far from my mind. When I decided at the end of 2019 that my quirky, fun post-apocalyptic webcomic would become novellas, I had almost a decade of thinking about the stories, characters, and world to put into this new vision for the series.

The names evolved, the way the characters talked changed, and while the core of the characters are the same, I was able to further refine their personalities.

Most of the dialogue from the original webcomic script made it into the novella: Sebastian and Meza's exchange about the Sols, much of the interaction between Sebastian and the old man, the bit about Chancy offering to cut Sebastian in on her scam. Even Chancy's habit of calling people "honey bun."

But I was able to expand the character interactions in super fun ways. Sebastian got to have a chat with a long-time listener, first-time caller. I gave Chancy the over-the-top entrance she deserved. And while the original script ends with Sebastian, Meza, and Chancy running from the monsters that were set loose, I gleefully added a big action sequence to the novella version.

Looking back on how the adaptation from comic script to novella turned out, I can truly say that I have no regrets about choosing this format.

And I'm beyond thrilled that you decided to give my

weird little book about a post-apocalyptic DJ a chance. As I think about the wealth of notes hastily scribbled down in my notebook back in 2010 (or was that 2011?), I snicker with conspiratorial glee while anticipating you reading all the funny, exciting, and heart-wrenching moments I'll be writing into future books.

That said, I hope you'll continue on this journey through the Midlands with me, Sebastian, Meza, and all the colorful characters you'll be meeting along the way.

K.C. Cordell
   California, July 2024

SOMETHING AWESOME JUST FOR YOU!

Psst… Psst! Yeah, you! Want a free book?

Maybe you're craving more…

- Super fun, loveable characters
- That quirky humor you now know and love
- Larger-than-life monster action

Get your hands on K.C. Cordell's epic fantasy novella, *Destroying a World Eater for Beginners* for abso-freakin-lutely FREE when you sign up for her Newsletter of Awesomeness!

Visit:
www.kccordell.com/newsletter
and start reading today!

A WEIRDO HAS ABDUCTED YARI TO HIS CREEPY LAIR AND
EXPECTS HER TO DO WHAT?!

SAVE THE WORLD, YOU PERV. GET YOUR HEAD OUT OF
THE GUTTER AND START READING

Yari of Inera is a nobody. No. She's less than that. A mouthy orphan who gets by on her street smarts and nimble feet, she knows her place. So when she's plucked from her ordinary life and brought to an eerie, colorless fortress to be told by a man on a throne that she's some chosen one, she isn't impressed. She's seen her share of grifts and tricks. This one's no different.

Only her abductor's tricks defy her best attempts to explain them away. But stubborn to a fault, Yari will require solid evidence before she believes anything this strange man says about a world eater coming to destroy the planet. Or her being the one to stop it

Unfortunately for her, irrefutable proof is exactly what her abductor has in mind. Even if it puts her directly in the path of a cataclysmic disaster that she is nowhere near ready to take on...

If you like surly mentors, smart-mouthed chosen ones, and big monsters with even bigger appetites, then this gripping action and adventure fantasy is right up your alley!

www.kccordell.com/newsletter

BTDUBS... WHO WROTE THIS BOOK ANYWAY?

L.A. native K.C. Cordell likes writing about aliens, monsters and superpowers. She attempted to write her first novel when she was nine. She didn't finish it, but it's still floating around. She read it recently. It's pretty good.

She likes reading and watching junk about aliens, monsters and superpowers too. Some of her favorite books and shows from growing up in the '90s include *Animorphs, Ella Enchanted, Gargoyles, Spiderman: The Animated Series,* and *Buffy the Vampire Slayer.* These inspired her to pick up a pen and their influence can still be seen in the writing she does today.

She hopes to one day own a t-shirt with an alpaca wearing an afro on it. If she ever got a puppy, she would name him Kiba. Thanks to once upon a time reading many, MANY books on the topic to her nephew, she's pretty good at pronouncing dinosaur names. Her favorite to say is pachycephalosaurus.

"Pachycephalosaurus."

Nice!

But she totally has to look up how to spell it.

Connect with K.C. on TikTok:
@bykccordell